GREETINGS FROM OZ

First published in the United Kingdom in 2014 by
Portico Books
10 Southcombe Street
London
W14 0RA

An imprint of Anova Books Company Ltd

ISBN 9781907554834

A CIP catalogue record for this book is available
from the British Library.

10 9 8 7 6 5 4 3 2 1

Printed and bound by 1010 Printing International Ltd, China

This book can be ordered direct from the publisher at
www.anovabooks.com

GREETINGS FROM OZ

SNAPSHOTS FROM THE ROADSIDE ...

PATRICK DALTON

PORTICO

You mustn't judge Australia by the Australians.
Dame Edna Everage

G'DAY!

The world holds a lot of preconceptions about Australia. People arrogantly tend to think that they already know the country even if they haven't been there. That was certainly my position before I visited to compile this book. To my shame my head was full of lazy stereotypical images of Australia farmed mainly from movies, TV shows, soap operas and, least helpfully, beer commercials. The Australia of my mind was made up of a loose concoction of images of men wearing hats with corks dangling off them, Amazonian women playing beach volleyball, koalas, kangaroos, extreme public drunkenness, the word 'dag', Harold Bishop playing the trombone, sun-bleached surfers and the whole 'throw another kookaburra on the barbie' thing. Each of these illusions turned out to be as far from the truth of the place as is possible.

The hats with corks thing I found only really exists in gift shops, although I could've done with one in Perth, a city that I took to be a natural magnet for people with severe physical ticks, until I strayed open-mouthed into one of the clouds of flies that bother the city in November, and realised what everyone else was doing.

Perhaps the greatest and most important of these illusions to be shattered for me was the notion that Australia is an example to the rest of the world on quality of life: a modern, tidy and wholesome place to live. I was relieved to find that if you scratch just beneath the surface, in places Australia can be just as crummy as anywhere else.

In my hunt for the unintentionally funny, for the depressing, for the questionable and the for the downright weird I spent a few weeks taking in as much of the country as possible. This mainly involved stopping in as many cities as I could, working my way clockwise around the edge of the country. Now should you be an Australian reading this, and I sincerely hope you are, you might need reminding, because you're almost certainly used to it by now, that your country is enormous. For someone like me who lives on a tiny island clinging to the edge of Europe it is almost unimaginably huge. The very idea of being able to take a six-hour flight and still being in the same country is astounding, as a six-hour flight in any direction from Europe can land you somewhere where the language, people and culture are bewilderingly different. That being said, subtropical Darwin felt as different as it could be to Perth, whilst Sydney and Melbourne both had very distinct characters of their own. Australia makes Europe seem very tiny, very crowded and very old by comparison.

The natural beauty Australia is famed for didn't feature in my experience as I didn't get to see any of it. This was probably completely the wrong way to see the country, but in doing it like this I hope I got to see a glimpse of what the real Australia is like: 89 percent of Australians live in urbanised areas. I spent my time endlessly criss-crossing each city and visiting as many neighbourhoods as possible on my quest for photos.

On my penultimate day in Australia, shortly after taking the photo which features on the front of this book, I had my first real encounter with the unique wildlife there. Unfortunately for me, and I suppose him, he was dead: a kangaroo lying by the side of the road. This seemed a strangely fitting end for my journey and as I looked down at the crumpled body of the strange creature that would usually be bouncing around like a carefree idiot I reflected on my time in Oz and thought to myself, 'What the hell have you been doing for the past few weeks? You've been looking for knob graffiti, misspelt signs, bad puns, dumb graffiti and scenes of despair like usual ... you fool. You need to come back and have a look at this place properly next time'. And you know what? I think I was right.

Inside this book I hope you'll enjoy the photos that show a humorous side to urban living in Australia. These photos take an affectionate look at the ill-conceived, the world of human error and also the unique Australian sense of humour.

Patrick Dalton
Australia, April 2013

Lifeguard knobism, Surfers Paradise

Well-placed sticker, Sydney

Poor Pete, Brisbane

Drug dealer improvises billboard, Newton

Well that's a novel excuse for
Metro not running, Melbourne

Stunned koala statue, Southport

Sofa's paradise, Surfers Paradise

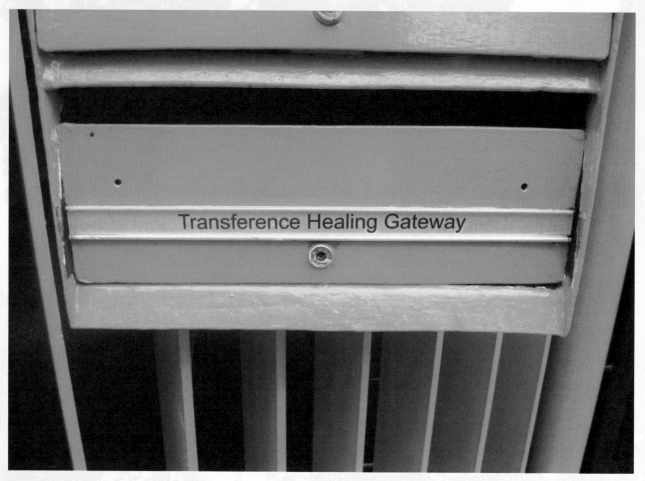

... or, as it's more commonly known, 'a letterbox', Sydney

Children beware! Northcote

Terrifying car, Mandurah

Sherlock Holmes lives!
Melbourne

Insert crude euphemism here,
Northcote

Market Rules, Fremantle

Adjust your expectations accordingly, Gold Coast Line

Gardening pun, Ringwood

Grammar snob, Brisbane

In a lifetime of decisions, this is your best? Gold Coast

Ignored instruction, Melbourne

Shocking sign, Sydney

Adapted sign, Sydney

Pavement penis, Perth

Violence-themed chip shop, Brisbane

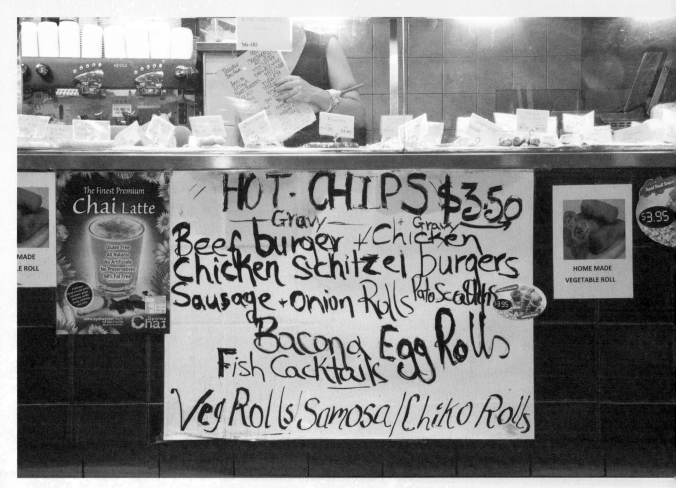

Fish Cacktails? Actually I'm not hungry, Sydney

Those are some serious activists, Brisbane

Baby Changing Station

Soiled nappy, Adelaide

City honours the caped
crusader, Melbourne

Unfortunately named coach, Great Ocean Road

Strangely apt, Melbourne

Sarcastic addition, Bondi Beach

The campaign for justice continues, Melbourne

The Boomerang School
Come on in

BACK IN 10 MINS

AMERICAN EXPRESS
Cards
Welcome

That's one slow boomerang, Sydney

Budget? I wonder why, Darwin

Excellent business name, Darwin

Bus stop, Brisbane

Untaken note, Darwin

If this is the future, then God help us all, Perth

Community notice, Sydney

Beware of the cows, Nerang

Unusual service, Manly

All the big news, Darwin

Cheery church poster, Fremantle

Wall beer, Melbourne

Clever graffiti ... or is it? Sydney

Fellatio statue, Brisbane

I'll take that as a 'no' then, Perth

Unnecessary gingerism, Brisbane

That's an order, Tingalpa

Make me an offer, Tingalpa

Don't mess with karma, Sydney

The van doth protest too much, Sydney

How to lose your own argument, Perth

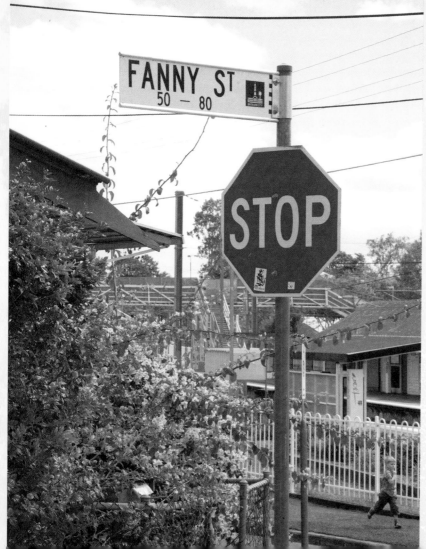

Snigger #1, Brisbane

Snigger #2, Melbourne

That's one way to save money I suppose, Melbourne

Lucky us, Nunawading

Someone isn't a fan, Nightcliff

Rudimentary mailbox, Melbourne

Worst. Park. Ever. Sydney

I beg to differ, Darwin

The helmet masks upset well,
Brisbane

Aborigine car sticker, Darwin

Disgruntled locals vandalise ugly building, Nightcliff

Anti-speed hump graffiti, Perth

Is Piggy on the menu?
Melbourne

"There will be no carbon tax under the government I lead."

Julia Gillard - Channel 10 News, 16 August 2010

Gillard is a Loser, Geelong

... really looks like you've been
stabbed, Brisbane

Unfortunately named
boutique, Sydney

Lawyers' sign, Mandurah

Road safety sign #1, South Australia Border

Blunt advertising, Sydney

Weirdest street name in Australia, Melbourne

Toilet instructions, Skenes Creek

High marks, Perth

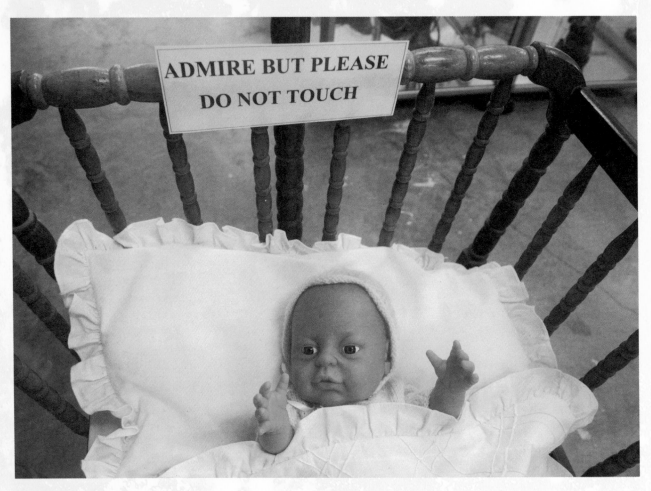

ADMIRE BUT PLEASE
DO NOT TOUCH

There's no danger of either of those things happening, Koroit

Anti-piss sign, Perth

Watch out for crocs! Darwin

Proud father, Sydney

Misleading sign, Sydney

PUSH

MON-SAT 9:00am-9:00pm
SUN/   10:00am-8:00pm
Open on public holiday

WARNING
No Cash Left On Premises
These premises are
protectected by Security CCTV

Extra security, Perth

Do NOT obey this sign, you will be prosecuted, Brisbane

Except the mobility scooter, obviously, Nunawading

Who wants helmet hair? Darwin

If you Run at this
wall hard enough
you will get
Hogwarts ♡

CAFE HOURS
MON-WED 8AM-11PM
THUR-FRI 8AM-1AM
SAT. 10AM-1AM
SUN 10AM-11PM

Do NOT try this, trust me on that,
Melbourne

Strange fruit, Perth

STOP!
PLEASE PLEASE,
DON'T
PISS
OR VOMIT
IN THIS DOORWAY!

LETTERS

Desperate plea, Sydney

Sadly poignant name, Brisbane

Bottle shop, St Kilda

Karaoke bar, Sydney

Sadly de-vandalised sign, Darwin

I GOT 🦀'S SEAFOOD CAFE

Unsurprisingly this place had closed down, Wynnum

Road safety sign #2, South Australia Border

Street bargain, Newton

Unusual punishment, Sydney

Kinky sign, Surfers Paradise

Liberal policies, right-wing 'tache,
Perth

City honours Superman's girlfriend, Sydney

Landing Nemo, Perth

... but 72 hours or larger
increments are fine, Northcote

Look up ... how to spell 'objects', Brisbane

Stair debate, Brisbane

Bondage-themed restaurant,
Sydney

Helpfully labelled tree, Darwin

To All fellow Tenants

Can we all be careful of who we are letting into the building. Every night last week and again tonight, I have found a bag lady sleeping in the stairwell.
Not only does she stink, but I caught her pissing (that's urinating) on the first fight of stairs tonight. That's the smell you can smell this morning!!!!

Can we please make sure that the door is closed behind you when coming in. Sometimes the door DOES not close properly.

She buzzes until someone lets her in. PLEASE IF YOU ARE NOT EXPECTING ANYONE DO NOT BUZZ THIS LADY IN!!!!!!

You're sincerely
Fellow Neighbour

Helpful definition, Sydney

Additional Photography

Sylvia Caddies, Stuart Silcox, Simon Gretton, Richard Castiel, Katja Forbes.

Thanks

Kevin and Sara Dalton for the beer, bed and the laughs; Tiph and Jordie Brown, the coolest couple in Oz; Earl Jay, an old friend in a new country; Stuart Silcox, a fellow afficionado of the shit; Richard Castiel for the insiders guide; and of course the excellent Malcolm Croft and Harri O'Neill at Anova for putting up with me, and for all their hard work over this series of books. Thank you.